Mind the Monkey

Pramod Shankar is a fish-loving career
nomad who grew up near the sea.
Pramod has been writing poetry
from his teen years, the quality of which
almost got him banned him from entering
his 6th grade English classroom.

His first book of poetry, *From the Terrace*,
was published by Writers Workshop,
Calcutta, in 2000. His poetry
has also appeared in the collections of
The British High Commission in India
and The Poetry Society. Pramod has also
published a book on alternative
healing for HIVAIDS.

Pramod organizes frequent poetry meets
called Poetry with Zac, which are
presided over by his Cocker Spaniel.
He lives in Bangalore, and runs a creative
consulting company called *The Story Loft.*

Pramod is married to Lakshmi, a home
chef, and has two children: Manasi
and Nishant.

Mind the Monkey

PRAMOD SHANKAR

BOOKSTHAKAM

Mind The Monkey (Poetry)

By: Pramod Shankar

www.pramodshankar.com
shootitifitrhymes.blogspot.com

Cover & page design, and typography by Shikhin P Vasu
Cover illustrations by TV Narayan

Price: ₹200/-

This Edition: January 2021

Published by: Booksthakam
4B Muthoot Rainbow Apartments
AKG Nagar Road, Peroorkada
Thiruvananthapuram 695005
E-mail: info@booksthakam.com
www.booksthakam.com

ISBN: 978-81-948170-7-9

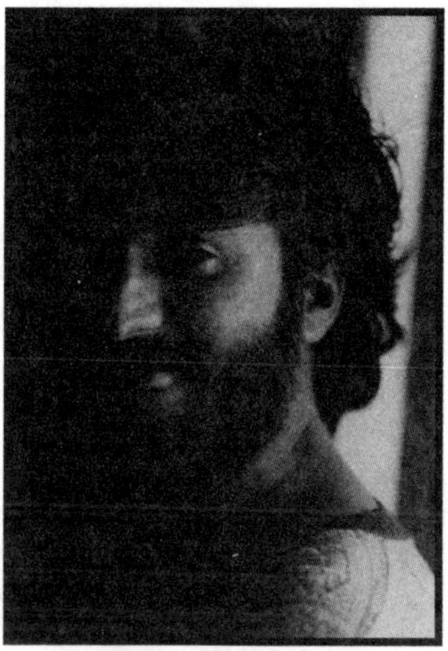

In the ever-loving
memory of TV Narayan,
my soul brother.

Foreword

Meeting Pramod is serendipity—an hour in his presence and you walk away bathed in the liquid sunshine of his wit, whimsy and kindness.

His poetry too has the same unforgettable essence. Warm and vivid, it shines a light on his deeply unique and yet relatable ideas and experiences.

Whether finding its way to you in the form of a sonnet, a haiku or a pick-up line, his poetry is a kaleidoscope reflecting a life well-lived with friends and family (and strangers too) and love and laughter (along with a due measure of tears). As it bounces merrily onwards, you'll find yourself sharing in the joys and sorrows it etches out.

I'm stopping short of comparing the poems in this volume to a summer's day, but only just, and only because I'm no bard. Instead, I'll let Pramod and his poetry take over.

Celia Vincent
7th September, 2020

Mind the Monkey

CONTENTS

CONTENTS

Mind the Monkey

Where does he go?
What does he touch?
Who does he bare
his sleaze-yellow teeth at?

What's his perch?
Rain-gobbled bark
of wilting mangosteen,
rotting leaves layered
with dead drying dung,
alabaster alcove, gilded spire,
driftwood dynasty
or mossy rooftop?

What does he hold?
Memories woven lazily
into gossamer globes,
luminous and warm?
Fear, singeing the skin
off barrels of wasted hope?

What does he speak?
Elegies bursting with manic laughter,
Sufi-words stranded as beads
on shiny rolling string,
incense swirling up, soothing
raw, ragged nerve-tips?

Mind, the monkey -
cageless, wanton, naked beast;
first to appear
and last
to leave.

Quay Notes

Some salt. A little water-lily smell.
A rust-drop from a forgotten anchor.
A coir strand, unspun from a rope, on a pier.
A horn that cuts through the steel-packed fog.
Grey mud that cascades
from a dredger's ballast.

Harbor.
Around the Chinese fishing nets,
listless men gather with little talk and less fish.
Hyacinth, cradling air-pockets to hearts,
speckle green into the grey waters.
A pink water-bottle floats,
trailing old school-tales. A bubble bursts.

A white boat, drunk with passenger-weight,
weaves down the bay.
The jetty stirs awake.
Baskets of fowl, fish, and bananas go aloft, suddenly.
Two gulls rake the sky with an off-key duet.
A kingfisher cuts a cameo.
From an old memory, a baby cries.

A bawdy song cuts in from the toddy shop.
Over a dish of pickled prawn,
a lifetime is shared.
Love and lust mingle in the toss
of a jasmine-scented plait.
The dredger honks.

Inside my shirt, an old sea-breeze blooms.

Three Slaps

Three slaps of the oar
Three slaps of canal water,
Green and alive and dark.

Three laps forward for the boat.

It's a long way to go, with
A heavy mind
Heavy limbs
And eyes that smell of soot.

A dead twig floats by.
A fish flashes its white belly.
A ship's horn, blunted
By the fog,
Probes through the dark.

A crab drums a dark litany
On a broken shell.

A shoe surfaces, carrying
Old footprints from a ballad.
Slowly, the water is deserted.

Doom sinks down,
Releasing a school
Of bubbles.

Shellspeak

Dawn brings the gulls out
white, crackling, cocky.
Salt, deep in the sea's sinews,
long for an eye.
In the depths of the fishing net
a lone mackerel gasps.
An old litany escapes
from the church's tired heart.

The harbor coats old wounds
with coarse salt.

Far away, a coffin closes.

Single File

How thick is your solitude?
Can it be cut with a butter-knife?
Would a pebble falling on it bounce back, or
make a dent?
Would it soak in the rain, like a weed would soak
in the sea?
Would it let the breeze through, or hoard it for a
rainy day?
Would it fill your halls like a haiku gone hoary,
or rustle in the corners with the
naphthalene fumes and the leftover
monsoon breath?

Would its echo stain the edges of your
coffee-mugs,
would its footprints pepper your rugs?

Would your solitude mumble? Stutter?
If it sings, would it be a tenor or a baritone?

Is it a soufflé, light and feathery, or a quiche,
crusty and crisp?
Would it ever snap like the edge of a benne
dosa?

As a blanket, would it quell like wool or lull like
satin?
Would it swell and shrink like the tide,
or wax and wane like the moon on your
bedroom window-pane?

Would it ever float out to me on a
sparrow's wings?

Swansong

Swans, simply silvered
from the stalactite mines
of yesterday's magnetic waters.

Swans.

Long necks in swooping grace
like heroines from a Russian novel
- feathers flouncy and shiny,
wind-tunnel-brushed-back tidy.

Swans.

Webbed feet making ploppy pictures
on marble floor.
Beaks outlining haughty arcs
in the monsoon-thick July air.
Sanguine eyes, beady and shallow,
probing like blunted bayonets.

Swans.

Arriving to sing,
departing with silence.

Offline

One after the other,
the birds came.
All white
all chaste
all blank.

One spoke of empty rhymes
and blind ballads
another, of blisters
that grew crimson with the setting sun.
One wept of feathers
lost in a molten barrage of scalded dreams
and yet another rested its beak in mire.
One said, "I've flown over rusted,
demented kingdoms
and blood-soaked flower beds".
His brother, with claws blunted
from perching long on sun burnt spikes,
remembered a drop of wild nectar.
One stepped out of line,
indecisive.

Meerkat's Dance

Sift the rumors through the slit
of the nib,
Sing your sermons backwards.
Wear that wet plastic raincoat
Over your bare, bruised skin
And read that testament.

It's grainy and grassy at the same time.
Fluid yet tentative, blindly turning
the rings on the number lock. Bleeding
an empty bleed, not quite red nor
visible. Yet viscous and singeing on skin.

Let the neurons collect under the porous,
night-time sky
And drop their leaden necks.
There must be a star somewhere,
reserved for sighting
on such moments.

Let's look skywards.

Question to an Artist who Killed Himself

For a moment and a half,
you cling.
Fingertips digging the precipice
of my skull
and as I close my eyes I see a kid
drooling in the ecstatic oblivion of madness.

What is it that you seek,
you ask me.
Through trillions of chafed sun-sets
robbing cake-shops
for crumbs with burnt edges
slanting, sleeting rain boiling
on raw burnt tin sheets
and the smell of singed flesh?

Masked trapeze.
Springing up from the safety net
the Big Top
ringmasters with cigarette-holders
a mile long
and pointed, pronged tails.

Why is it that you paint your face,
you ask me.

With white and vermillion
and a grin with curling corners
and the skull of a mouse for a nose?

Why is it that you
paint?

In Absentia

Please remember
to feed the fish.

Water the flower beds.
Remember to rake

the golden brown leaves
on the driveway.

Fluff the pillows;
wipe the rain water seeping onto
the blue marble floor.

Make the doves feel at home.
Lead the rooster to a worm
every other day.

Pat the cats, bathe the dogs, air the carpets.

If my memories come calling,
just turn away.

Current Feelings

The saddest water
I found in the canal.
Green, a burnt green
of snubbed-out desire.
Thick, murky aftertaste
of layered longings.
Twigs and seeds, feathers and shells
melting between grinding planes
of current.

Salt from unspent tears
feeding ugly, lethargic, unforgiving,
smirking, whiskered fish.

Then, from nowhere,
an Amber glow falls.

Painshore

Every day I take a long winding walk
on the shores of disease.
People I meet smile
and make pleasant talk.
"What color is your pain today",
an old woman asks.
A white dog wags its tail
a baby cries softly
a bird hoots.
I walk on.

In the tea-stall,
a smiling man offers tea.
In his glass cupboard,
deep-fried bananas reflect
the sunset glow.
I seek you

in the sand speckled with baby sea-shells
in the wind that breathes salt
in the sky that slowly starts to bleed.

I walk on.

Damp

Rain.
The city is one grey damp huge slushy
wet blanket.
The sun sprinkles powdered light
that gets filtered and scattered
miles above.
Wet crows, wet bullocks, wet
dreams shelter the hearts of damp memories.

Morning.
Face up on a park bench
granite digging backbone,
tamarind leaf canopy superimposed
on grey clouds.
Why does cloud 21 take the shape
of your nose?
Why does the pie-dog's white patch
remind me of an old holiday?

Life's questions are beyond me
today.

Rain Tree

You've visited my house, yes, many times,
But have you seen my rain tree?
The one with clouds for leaves
rainbows for fruits and little droplets for seeds?
Come with me, touch it.
Shake its branches, let the crystal drops descend on you.
See how wet the roots are.
See the damp bark, the rain-filled hollows
And the gum-mingled resin
trickling from the pores.

This is my rain tree
this is my me.
Don't hurt it, please,
even with a blade.

Searing Sunrise

The salty boomerangs in the nerve-endings
tingle
like a blade does,
just before slicing through thin veins.

The growl starts, silently first, moving into a
roar
that drowns the peaks of torment
sparking up the oceans of pure throb.

'Die, man, die when you still can', an honest
broken slivered voice speaks.
Rain, descending from the grey masses of
waylaid dreams, glistens in assonance.
Drops fall off, touch the sinews of another
sunrise of pain
and evaporate.

Another dawn arrives on red-hot tongs.

White Ebony

Some days,
you scrape the
sand off the
sandpaper.

Some days, the
fins off the
shark
take over
as door-stoppers.

Some days,
eyelashes are dams
shredded by
white-hot, angry
gales.

Some days,
shave-foam seeps
right into the pores
and wets
the larynx.

Some days,
metal tries to cut water
and draws sparks.
Manhole covers fly
like frisbees.

Some days,
black's a shade lighter
than white.

Re-coil

Serpent, you may have the last laugh.
While the maggots are dense
with their brainy little waltz,
while the dark eggs' hatchlings
go blind before birth,
while the eels turn magenta
from touching raw corals,
you may crackle in purple-venom-laden
glee.

Serpent,
who knows what your thoughts are?
Dreams wet, shiny and dripping,
rhyming with scalesong
as you walk.
Memories rising in slithery smoke
while grass-blades shrug in wet revolt.

Serpent,
be
my
guest.

Conspiracy

God was in a benign mood.
He said, take my diamond mines
To park your thoughts.
Close to the core of the earth,
Where old secrets jostle
The fire of my loins.

God was in a forgiving mood.
He said, come sit on the apex
Of my shoulders, where the Everest breathes
Silence into the breaks between clouds
And rest awhile.

God was in a relaxed mood.
He said, come keep your heart
In my valley of flowers,
Let it cool with the dew
From the slumbering tulips and daisies.

God was in an indulgent mood.
He said, let me soothe your face
With a shimmer of silk, the breath of cherubs
And a serenade of peacock feathers.

I said,
Let me lay my thoughts on a park bench.
Let me perch on the step outside
the washroom.
Let me keep my heart in a parking lot, and
Let my face be soothed by a reckless
monsoon drop.

God looked over my shoulder
At you
And smiled.

No Thanks

Not for me,
the half-imagined whiff
of a comforting breath.
Not for me, concern gift-wrapped
with a bright satin bow.
Not for me,
the safety of installments.

Come to me with all the tact
of a baby gorging on a breast.
Come to me with all the restraint
of the rain racing to wet the earth.
Pick my brains
shred my skull
devour my guts like warm brown sausages
and pound my blood to crimson your
forehead.

If you don't feel like it,
please,
vanish now.

Listen?

Maybe it's a little dark corner
of a forgotten dream.

Maybe it's a thinning strand
from a satin drawstring.

Maybe it's gum, cracking
on the bark of a graying tree.

Maybe it's a grain
from an old footprint
on a silver beach.

Maybe it's the eroding lead
from a pencilled love-note.

Maybe it's the blunt sparkle of a moon
stone,
seen through frosted glass.

Maybe it's the last raindrop in a monsoon
puddle,
about to evaporate.

Maybe it's your voice,
still alive,
from another world.

Magic

Let me keep my magic
Hidden
Under your eyelashes.

Let me keep it
Damp and silent
Between your thumb and forefinger.

Let me bring it to you
Silently in your sleep
And leave it to nestle
Inside your navel.

Let me mould it
With my drunken fingers
Twisting wisps of old hangovers
Dipped in Haiku juice.

Let me slip it in
When nobody's watching...
Especially you.

Steam

A gust of hot shower,
like the first June drops of rain.
In the shower stall, mist and breath merge
like tongues seeking lust-bubbles.

A jaw clamps a shoulder, raising alarm
on the soap-stream sliding down from the neck.
A hand
- opening, closing, tracing, moving -
trails down a goose-bump, then cups.

On a lone soap-dome, a tiny rainbow bursts.
Its ghost slithers down the chin, the neck;
rests in a tiny hollow, gets split by a nestling hair.
Firm softness pulses to the rising rhythm
of hearts' beats.
A voyaging shampoo-drop snuggles
into a navel.

Higher above, an eyelash trembles.
A word, unsure and unchristened,
reflects on a sigh, retreats.
A loofah, aided by trembling fingers,
finds a mate in a valley.

Heat, having left the shower, reaches for the
sinews.
A tiny muscle twitches on a glistening calf.
A wandering nail resurrects
a forgotten pore.

On the floor, wetnesses meet in slippery silence.

Home

Three wilted asters
droop down from the bin,
serenely.

An ancient Mercedes
suns itself
under the tamarind tree.

Salted beef, rotting lettuce
and Simla apples
blend fragrances.

A lone mouse,
tired from a long moonlight scavenge,
retracts into its hole.

Fresh biscuits, brown, warm and crusty,
line the pan at Chai Day.

In the fish stall,
shark and tuna, shankara and mullet,
pomfret and rohu
rub fins in heavenly unity.

The happily mentally challenged man
shuffles by; grin, twinkle in eye,
and wicker basket intact.

Asifbhai smiles
and sunshine descends.

Johnson Market.

Kaiku Haiku?

It drips
from the edges
of a blunt dagger.

It churns
the insides
of a rusty boiler.

It slithers
in the depths
of a stinking sewer.

It moistens
the sweat-streams
between skin and moving skin.

It weeps
in the blackness
of a windowless mind.

It laughs
from the tip
of an infant's pink toe.

The poem.
Everywhere.
Disguised.
Devious.

Made in China

Latif Bhai cuts the metal strips.
Ganesh and Giridhar sharpen their sides to
knife-edges.

D' Souza picks the junglewood bits,
sells them to Peer Mohammed
who sizes them down to knife handles.

Nair mates metal knife and wooden handle
on his attic work-bench.
As Ammini sharpens each against the spinning
stone wheel,
sparks fly.
Their son, Pravin, trims all the edges,
adds the rivets and cleans the knives.

Rashid Bhai mounts the crate, packed with
knives
onto his green Raleigh bicycle
and trundles around, galli-galli.
Leela Behn touches, feels, pats, bends, twists,
haggles,
and buys one.

In another part of the city,
legions of precisely made stainless steel knives
made in a Kaizen-certified factory
glisten in a supermarket's
fluorescent light.

Feelers

For a change,
Let us touch
With our bodies.

Lay bare our hungry skins
Reach for slippery corners
(not of our minds, this time)
And feel a different fulfillment
Rise.

Let us journey on different wings
Cling to different cliffs
Ease a different rhythm
Tease a different ink

Leave Kant for contentment
Keats for heat
Brecht for breast
Sinclair for sin

And roll up some grass
In a page of Grass
Afterwards.

Brown Eyes

The baker said, I want brown.
Sin-steeped chocolate sauce,
Caramel crusty and burnt,
Cashew roasted to an infinite dark.

The painter said,
I want brown.
Raw umber, tempered
With a downy fawn and spiked
With shots of bronze.

The chef said,
I want brown.
The goo off the overdone sausage,
The edge from the cinnamon stick,
The fat from the greased
Old turkey.

The farmer said,
I want brown.
Early light glinting off the wheat
The patch between the calf's little horns
Bushels ripe in silent wait
And twilight.

Then you opened your eyes
And all fell silent.

Then and Now

Some day, I'll collect your tears
in a thimble
and wash away the salt,
drop by crystal drop.

Some day, I'll stop a raindrop
in flight
and steal its sparkle
to light up your eyes.

Some day, I'll make a little windmill
that turns
with your sighs
and breathes out rainbows.

But meanwhile,
Pass the tomato sauce, please.

Tonight

Tonight, let me talk to the moon
silently.

Tonight, let me weave a prayer
with strands of silken guilt
and breathe it to the stars
silently.

Tonight, let me walk the dew-kissed path
and crumple the autumn leaves
silently.

Tonight, let me hold a warm, threadbare memory
kiss a lost, lingering thought
caress the feel of a pulsing brow
silently.

Tonight, let me endure your absence
silently.

Return to Sender

Meekly, let the doors close behind us.

Let the forlorn templates with caving margins
suck us into their vortex.
Let crimson dissolve in the deeper
finger-reaches
And let Bolton sing,
"Can I touch you there".

Let the earth's clitoris erupt a shattering
thunderstorm and let all the birds fly away
to Ithaca.

As silence settles, let me say my last prayers.

You, my friend, can watch from behind your
misty glasses.

Reminder

Did you ever know
there's a handful of snow
with my name etched on the verge?

Did you know the gale that filled your raincoat
had a mouthful of my breath?

Did you see my eyes glint
in the puddle
that splashed mud under your step?

Could you, my friend, lift your tongue
to the hail that raced
with my pulse?

Did you, but once, feel the sweat
from the lone ray that signals my lust?

Did you ever touch the sand
warm with my last regret?

Move gently on, close your eyes.
Death has my name on its lips.

Satin

Maybe a small, in fact miniscule,
lavender bouquet for your birthday.
A sweet-smelling,
feather-furry-felt-downy,
soft medley of whispers
gift-wrapped in orange blossoms.

Maybe a journey
into the centre of your eyeballs
honey and treacle, melted
smooth-flowing into
your memories.

Maybe a brush
against your breast
dragonfly wings fluttering
on butter.

Maybe a glance, framed in guilt
maybe a touch
maybe a word
maybe a whole belated lifetime.

One More Twirl

Is there a waterfall where you come from?

A tiny whirlwind that touches the edge your sanity,
like the breath of a dark animal
that you dreamt about...
the one you saw dart across the hay field.

Is there a wood fire, safe in the cocoon of your mind
an ember that you'll save for a rainy thought...
Is there one last longing before I leave?

See the last lead leave the love-note
the last grain leave an old foot-print
the last feather descend your spine

Turn the page, but slowly love
Let your fingertip seek one last, last waltz.

Outercourse

Where's my free fish,
She asked me again,
where the fish is my friggin' free fish?

I'd left it on the ledge,
I said,
with the rainbow and the prunes,
maybe the rain came
and washed it away.

Where did you leave all that kindness, she asked,
the kind of which I thought will never dry away?

I'd left it for you
on the garage window-sill
maybe a thief came and
took it away.

Where are your words with the slur
and the salt, where is your tongue with
its sly, gilded tip?

I'd left it all for you,
just hanging loose –
maybe ol' Spot came
and licked it away.

Cat Trap

And then, the cat-trappers came.
Large, netted cat-bags in hands
cat-whistles attached
to necks, with dog-tags;
identity and shrill instrument
in one fabric loop.

Cats sensed the intruders,
the impending doom;
paws poised mid-move,
whiskers trembling, eyes darting
half-finished meows frozen
in the summer air.

Cat-trappers.
Anti-feline squad
in rubber footwear, tails bristling
like antennas,
annihilators of the Siamese,
tabbies
and the common house-proud
kitties.

Stealthy stalkers
lethal demolishers
determined bellers all.

No, Tom

Take your hands off the raincloud,
Tom, God told Thomas;
Go wring that towel you dropped
into the pool.

Leave my twilight alone, Tom,
God told Thomas;
Light a candle and pray.

Don't wipe your soles on my prairie grass,
Tom, God told Thomas;
Load them with grains from the sand-pit.

Don't eye my lotus stems, don't chase my
backwater ducks, don't covet
that little squirrel's tail fur.

Don't play my broken reeds, Tom.
Play the drum that you left behind.

Ode to the *Sulaimani*

Cheap tea leaves
One-quarter lime
One mint leaf, probably
unwashed.

A tiny glass with slats running
up half-way
One blackened pan
One tiny kitchen.

Ten grubby fingers
One large heart.

Insha Allah,
The *Sulaimani* lives on.

Weekend Wist

Why does the weekend
Bring in its wake
Wishes and wrinkles,
Promises and pauses?

When all I know
I need is
Your touch
If only for a millisecond.

Koshy's, Saturday Night

The red checked tablecloth
always plays tricks.
Eyeball always gets stuck
on the white squares. Funny.

Squint, and I swear, I see
a desolate gondolier, prying
open a treasure-box
full of dead rats.

Sewer
water creeps up through the
red squares. Dark, damp
patterns happen
like shoulder-cuts and rumps
of slaughtered pork.

Life
Ceases on the table as a plate is
laid,
really and truly.
A sheet of white paper
follows.

You can write an ode
even to a misguided
trout, the tablecloth
says. The thought
lingers.

Plan for a Sunset

The thin gay man in
the glistening tank top
and tight golden trunks
sways.

Bollywood blares. A
suspended raindrop
threatens to baptize
an over-ripe pear.
A gull calls, from
a distance. He sounds
thirsty.

I make plans for
the impending sunset. Let's
have an overdose
of Indigo this time,
I tell God.

Over the choppy
waters,
the sea chuckles.

Sanyukta

Cherub mine,
your curls are question marks
to a world losing its rainbows.

Deep in your eyes,
a drop of nectar cuddles
a world that fled my world
long ago.

And your smile.
A swing from papa's twinkle
to amma's warmth.
A hammock next to God.

Sanyukta.

Maybe someday,
I will tell you how
papa and I shared a smoke
as the rain-tree baptized both of us.

How amma and I sparred
on the wings of a practical joke.

But till then,
I shall just watch
the dimples
on your knuckles.

Attic

An old 'Brother' typewriter,
with the space key missing.
A snuff-box full of dust
and cockroach-wing flakes.
A half-decayed pack of Passing
Show cigarettes,
its damp, moth-eaten mascot
with its smile intact.

An old gale, trapped
in an ink bottle, scrapes the
blue scales one last time.
Its identity is remembered.
A silverfish peeks from page 97,
browned and dog-eared,
from Chekov.
It leaves a keyhole-shaped cavity
on the pastoral Russian landscape.

Two fingertips, one brown and one fair,
share a millimeter of electricity.

From a distant childhood,
two mothers call:
"What are you two doing up there?"

Downstream

A smile.
A bud of fluffy drool
on the lip-tip.

Tongue a pink rosebud.
Eye a sky full of fireworks.

A slow step. Falter.

A chubby foot, a bit like a sixties sedan,
up in the air.
Fat rounding up and falling
around the waist
in slow motion.

My index fingers out –
hands come and grip them.

A pause.
Then, the sparkling, saline,
amber shower hits my face.
My son has made a mark.

Mammorabilia

Which one will she favor today?

Blue, red and with polka dots?

Metallic grey, with frayed straps,
and smooth around the edges?

Lacy and white, like two prayer caps?

Pointed, envious, sun-blanched twins,
like Everest and Annapurna?

Blue, giving way, like old tea strainers?

Looking at the clothesline,
my cup runneth over.

Man Hood

Today, I will not shift to baritone
Every time a lady calls.

I will not pretend to be watching Formula 1
While my eyes are on Nigella Lawson.

I will help Mrs. Rangaswami across the street
Even while nobody's watching.

I will not let rage descend
If a little Nano overtakes my big Chevy.

I will not cringe
when my sister asks me to get her
a fresh box of Whisper Ultra XLs.

I will listen to the maid.

I will inhale deeply, the aromas of Cerelac
In wispy baby hair.

Today I will be more of a man
And less of a MAN.

Excuse me,
How do I reach Jayanagar 3rd Block?

Sibling Revelry

You 1961
Me 1962

You iced tea
Me rum, Coke, rum

You natural leader
Me natural dropout

You Allen Solly
Me street seconds

You lamp
Me shade

You birthday
Me candle

Departed Wet

In the moonlight
the ghost got an erection.
But its shadow,
being modest,
just blurred itself
and took a cold shower.

A Chef's Pick-up Line

Are you Rosemary,

or am I

wasting

my thyme?

Flotsam

Lightships do not bleed,
Says the old man in the
Wooden boat.

As the water-crabs claw sunsets
Back into their throats,
The sea reaches for a blade
To slit their unsuspecting skins.

Serene hyacinth, monk
Of the monsoon waves,
Drums a dirge
On the rainbow-crowned
backwater drops.

Six feet deep into the bay,
The dolphins dream
Of a lost quay.

Neptune's Visit

Mom always liked the fish-man.
Simple rain, without the accompaniments of
thunder, lightning and water-logging,
often delayed the fish-man.
Even kept him away for days.

Then the sun would peep out one day,
grinning through the jack-fruit leaves,
wicked.

The fish-man's bicycle horn
would startle the sparrows.

What ma? Sardines eh? Buy buy.
Your fry is magic. Also curry, pickle,
moiley, stew, roast, all full magic.

Baby in America, Singapore, Dubai,
all will love.

Mom, charmed to the gills,
would buy sardines, mackerel,
and black pomfret.

Self-doubt in F-minor

I like having a drink
On my own,
Elbows on the greasy pinewood table-top.
Like having a meal
Alone, watching the kitten
Fight its shadow.

Am I weird?

I love it when my exes'
Kids have kids,
I forget the wedding dates
Of in-laws' cousins,
Can't make a decent coffee
And let my dog with his dirty feet
On to the bed.

I keep confusing mint leaves
With coriander
Buy unnecessary hundred-rupee trinkets
Drink gin with my son
And quietly write my will.

If there is an exam
To get on to the pedestal,
I guess I would be
an F minus.

Let Us

One day, beloved,
Let's measure the path
From sand to sky,
From moonbeam to sun-ray,
From shark-fin to eagle-crest.

Let's hold each other
By our little fingers, and
Dream together
Till the gripe water
From our babyhoods blend.

Let's lie on our backs
On sawdust, counting
The feathers on each pink
Cloud.

Let's lie on our faces
On a whale-back fountain,
Waltzing, for a change,
With our eyelashes.

Let us.

Under the Siesta

Aluminium
discarded
angelic and reflective
catches a glint of saintliness.

Spry as a caterwauling neon sign,
it settles
before splitting
lengthwise.

Froth.
From the needles to the pines,
the swamps to the sled-tracks,
it reigns.

Spilled over from bilious exhausts;
made, shrewdly, by the
white-clad, scheming, roof-light-laden
tramplers of pride.

Let's light a fuse,
the imbecile says.
The wise spit on his sentence
with a studied snarl.

Sockless

I've never seen you
in socks.

Flip-flops, sandals, boat shoes...
always.
Or, nothing at all.

When did you last
wear socks?

Not at a business meet,
not at a wedding.
Maybe in your school,
which I had never stepped into.

Today, I look up
and wish
for your feet
at my door,
sockless.

Silent Monsoon

Remember the sand that boiled
in our hands as we dug into the earth
together?

Remember the chain
that stretched to its limit
when we pedaled hard on
our cycles?

Remember the shards
of skin that fell off
our knees, blending
into the soil, becoming
the feed
of earthworms?

Remember the round stains
our lassi glasses made
on the housefly-ridden
café counter?

Remember the future
that had crept in stealthily
into our words,
as we talked about
those high-flying glow-worms?

As I had smoked that
one Gold Flake King,
drinking the tea you had made
from a glass tumbler,
you had watched the raindrops
fall on the banana leaves
and roll off quietly.

Now, only the puddles remain,
and their song is lost
in the monsoon.

Jazz Bar

The smoke, blue-white and twirling,
Hits a spot on the naked 100-watt bulb.
A spotlight lingers lazily
Above the overfed leather couch.
From the brassy, bent trumpet,
A fleeting, blinding highlight hits the eye.

Jazz bar.

Grainy elegies, misty songs of
Dreams slaughtered and buried headless,
Odes to love
Splintered before birth.

Play the last one again,
Choruses the audience,
Lost in a reverie
Of journeys inward.

It's never the same song,
The players say.

As I walk away, I carry
A broken boom-box
Deep in my sinews.

Wrinkle

Meeting you in the hallway of pretensions,
I notice how you look so out of place.

You break your steps for a drink of water
from the mud-pot in the corner.

The crow watches.
You step over the shadow of the minaret that creeps
In from across the road onto the floor.
It tingles as it gets the breeze, rustled down from the folds
Of your sari.

Tell me, what did you think of all my lies
When I had told them to you?
What do you think of them
Now?

Did you ever see anything at all
In my gray and shameful ramblings,
In the repainted tin toys that
I had kept on your doorstep
And window-sill?

As we lay, face down, on the cold ugly mosaic floor
With mismatched tiles,
Did your heart ever keep a feather
Over one of mine?

All our kisses we never tasted,
The hands we never held,
The wrinkles we never etched in the grey, badly-embroidered sheets,
The goodbyes said early, the hellos whispered with hope
And hung to dry in the monsoon sun,
The touches born of a hunger that never left its safe dark space...
All speak to me in Braille today.

I close my eyes, my tongue, my ears,
My skin, my nail-tip,
Saving for another rainy day that will never arrive.

Flicker

In your race to the pine-trees,
Did you trample the little
Green mushroom?

You may have felt a soft squish
Beneath your boot;
A tiny crack
Like a toad's jaw breaking.

You stepped up and away,
Your eye on the firefly
That hovered over a cannabis bush.

I,
A veil of silverfish over my head,
Just stood
And watched.

Way to go

Yes, all entry sealed.
Steel dust ground into contacts
sentries guarding heart,
posted at each valve and ventricle.
Filters over ear drums,
deodorizers in nostrils,
number locks with Swahili numerals
on chastity belt.

Maybe I should try breaking into
Fort Knox instead.

Flood

Water splits muscles
smithereens concrete dams
lasers the pride of generations of
unseeinguncaringunmoving
imbeciles.

The children will never know
what split the water.
One half life,
the other, death.
One half Amrut
the other, Arsenic.
Children, dogs, grandmothers,
earthworms,
squirrels and butterflies will,
even after the flood,
blindly believe in water.

The rest will
get flushed.

The Amber Cellar

I had a friend
who used to tear
the edges off evenings
and weave mats
out of them.

He was a good man. He locked up
his evening-mats safely in the cellar
of his own house.

We used to marvel at
the strips of evening-edges
turning into the warp and weft of the mats.
Soon, evenings laced with a palette
of scarlet, amber, saffire, saffron,
and emerald green, became mats;
piled high one on top of another
resting upon the floor of his cellar.

But,
the insides of the cellar
which sheltered the mats
were filled with darkness.

Those who sauntered by,
Seeking the tones of
a lilting flute, birdsong,
twilight mantras, and adhans
were greeted by a deafening silence.

My friend departed
a few days ago, leaving behind
his evening-strip mats.

Just the other day, the wind swept by,
bringing back some evenings from the past.

None of them had
edges.

Foundation

I am a house held together with cello-tape.
Glass panes tacked together
with Blutac and bubblegum,
Fused, naked light-bulbs laden with
forgotten sparkle.

I am the driveway of hairline, moss-laden cracks
and drainpipes that believe they are not clogged.

I am the hinges, peppered with rust, singing off-key.
I am the rain, racing down the shingles;
The moss, getting clingy in old age.

I am the doorknob that has lost its turn,
the cellar where insomnia hits the bottle
and fans that trade stories about
failed suicide attempts.

I am the carpet, once red, threadbare,
laid out for stilettos.

A Grain of Sand

There may come a time
When you may not find me in your
mind's mirror.

You'll look at me, or through me,
Like an owl may look at an old brown leaf,
and move on.

Thoughts of me may not fill your leisure hours;
They may not even enter your mind at all.
As the milkman comes, the newspaper is folded back,
The sheets are swapped the mobiles charged,
Your mind may let go of things
Once deemed precious.

A grain of sand is important
Only when it is lodged
Within the eyelid.

In My Garden

Within the petals of my pain
lies a dewdrop that glistens to your light.

The petal, its veins, its barely-there fibres,
the oyster-white walls
that breathe tender, baby-breath life –
lie in wait quietly for the pink pulse
of that precious, curving finger-tip.

Moments, seconds, minutes, centuries rise
and ebb gently; patiently
as the rock that wears away for the wave
that never comes.

Time and tide cut hollows, hone crests,
fill crescents as rain feeds the moss.

Within the seeds of my pain, you lie
as a lost heartbeat within a golden grain.
Washed by the rains, but never washed enough
to soak in the breath of life.

I write in the sand, again and again,
my dry words that drink in
the salt
to fill their wounds.

Wait

The old, worn tablecloth at Koshy's
also waits for Rohini Venkatesh Malur.

The red squares -
bleached by years,
and fluorescent light
and the weight of elbows of varying girth
and tender coconut soup (no longer served here)
and meandering conversations
and silences
and mobile radiation
and causes
and theories
and insinuations -
are now a bleating shade of pink.

On the neighbour's laptop, one reads,
'Drones will soon deliver packages'.

Everyone waits.

Spring Cleaning

Layers off.
Clothes.
Skin.
Bone.
Marrow.
Guts.

What was left
flew out
through the window.